The Robodog

Frank Rodgers has written and illustrated a wide range of books for children: picture books, story books, how-to-draw books and a novel for teenagers. His work for Puffin includes the highly popular *Intergalactic Kitchen* series and the picture books *The Bunk-Bed Bus* and *The Pirate and the Pig*, as well as the best-selling *Witch's Dog* titles. He was an art teacher for a number of years before becoming an author and illustrator. He lives in Glasgow with his wife and two children.

Some other books by Frank Rodgers

THE WITCH'S DOG

THE WITCH'S DOG
AT THE SCHOOL OF SPELLS

THE WITCH'S DOG
AND THE MAGIC CAKE

THE WITCH'S DOG
AND THE CRYSTAL BALL

THE INTERGALACTIC KITCHEN SINKS

Picture Books
THE BUNK-BED BUS
THE PIRATE AND THE PIG

Frank Rodgers
The Robodog

PUFFIN BOOKS

PUFFIN BOOKS

Published by the Penguin Group
Penguin Books Ltd, 80 Strand, London WC2R 0RL, England
Penguin Group (USA) Inc., 375 Hudson Street, New York, New York 10014, USA
Penguin Group (Canada), 90 Eglinton Avenue East, Suite 700, Toronto, Ontario, Canada M4P 2Y3
(a division of Pearson Penguin Canada Inc.)
Penguin Ireland, 25 St Stephen's Green, Dublin 2, Ireland (a division of Penguin Books Ltd)
Penguin Group (Australia), 707 Collins Street, Melbourne, Victoria 3008, Australia
(a division of Pearson Australia Group Pty Ltd)
Penguin Books India Pvt Ltd, 11 Community Centre, Panchsheel Park, New Delhi – 110 017, India
Penguin Group (NZ), 67 Apollo Drive, Rosedale, North Shore 0632, New Zealand
(a division of Pearson New Zealand Ltd)
Penguin Books (South Africa) (Pty) Ltd, Block D, Rosebank Office
Park, 181 Jan Smuts Avenue, Parktown North, Gauteng 2193, South Africa

Penguin Books Ltd, Registered Offices: 80 Strand, London WC2R 0RL, England

puffinbooks.com

First published 2001

015

Frank Rodgers copyright © 2001
All rights reserved

The moral right of the author/illustrator has been asserted

Printed in China by RR Donnelley Asia Printing Solutions Ltd.

British Library Cataloguing in Publication Data
A CIP catalogue record for this book is available from the British Library

ISBN 978-0-141-31030-5

Gary and Sue stared out of the
window.

"Oh, no!" cried Gary. "Dad's just patted
the dog next door!"

"Quick, cover the jigsaw!" yelled Sue as
their dad came in.

It was too late.

"A-a-a-atchoo!"

Dad's sneeze was like an explosion and suddenly there was a jigsaw blizzard.

"Dad!" groaned Gary. "Why did you pat Rex? You know you're allergic to dogs."

His dad sighed and wiped his nose.
"I know," he said. "But I like dogs."

"So do we,"
said Sue.

"But we can't have one in case you
sneeze the house to bits."

"Sorry," said Dad. He sat down glumly. "What a morning," he sighed.

"I've just been to the police station. I lost my wallet and went to see if it had been handed in. But it hadn't."

Everyone jumped and spun round.

A plume of
green smoke was
drifting up from
the garden shed.

"That noise came from Mum's workshop!" cried Sue. "We'd better go and see what's happened."

They rushed out of the kitchen and ran towards the shed ...

... just as Mum popped her head out, her hair smoking slightly.
"I've finished it," she said proudly.
"What?" asked Dad.

"Oh, didn't I tell you?" said Mum. "I've been working on a robot."

"A robot?" gasped Gary. "What kind of a robot?"

Mum smiled. "A dog," she said.
"A robodog!" chorused Sue and Gary.
"Correct!" said Mum. "I call him Chip. Come on in and say hello."

In the centre of the floor stood the robodog. He was made out of bits of metal and plastic. He had hinges for ears and a toothbrush for a tail. Chip looked at them and his tail wagged with a faint click, click, click sound.

WOOF!

he barked in a tinny, crackly kind of way.

Gary and Sue laughed in delight.

"He's brilliant, Mum!" cried Sue.
"Totally!" agreed Gary.

Dad's nose twitched and he pulled out a
hankie.

"A-a-a-a-" he began
to sneeze, then
stopped and
blinked.

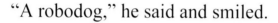

"A robodog," he said and smiled.

"Looks like I'm
not allergic to
this kind of
dog!"

Chip's tail wagged faster ...

CLICLICLICLICLICLICK!

Gary and Sue knelt down and patted
him.

"He's so cute!"
cried Sue.

"He's really cool!" agreed Gary. "Mum, you're so clever. We've got a dog at last!"

He stroked the robodog's back.
"Hello, Chip," he said.

Chip stood up on his hind legs and
panted.

"H-h-h-h-h-hello," he said.
Gary and Sue nearly fell over in
surprise.

"He said hello!" squeaked Sue.

She looked at
Mum in delight.
"Does that mean
Chip can talk?"

Mum grinned and nodded.
"Chip's computer brain is specially
programmed," she said. "It means he
can learn new things just like you do."

"And he has!" cried Sue. "He's just learned how to say hello!"

"Wow!" said Gary, patting the robodog's head.

"Say something else, Chip."

WOOF!

barked Chip and everyone laughed.

"I don't think he'll talk all the time," said Mum. "You have to remember that he's really programmed to be a dog ... even though he can do things that other dogs can't."

Chip trotted past them and went into the garden and Mum watched anxiously to see what he would do.

Through his *super-see* video screen, the robodog looked around at the house, trees and flowers.

Suddenly he caught sight of his tail.

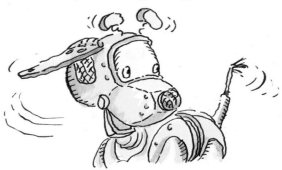

"Woof!" he
barked and tried
to catch it.

Round and
round went Chip ...

faster and faster
until he was
only a blur.

"Wow! If he goes any quicker he'll take
off," said Sue.

Suddenly Chip stopped and sniffed the air with his *super-sniff* nose sensors.

Selina, next door's cat, was watching from under a bush.

"Sssssss," hissed Selina, flashing her claws and trying to scare Chip away.

WOOWOOWOOWOOF!

barked Chip and bounded forward
fearlessly.

RAAAOOOOWL!

yowled Selina in surprise and scooted
over the garden fence.

Chip stopped and grinned. Being a dog
was great fun!

Mum was delighted.
"He works
perfectly!" she said.

Dad smiled. "Yes ... Chip might
sometimes talk like a person ... but he
certainly acts like a dog!"

"You don't call that thing a dog, do
you?" said a snooty voice.

21

Everyone looked up to see Mr and Mrs Minted, their next-door neighbours, peering over the fence.

Mrs Minted held Selina in her arms and Mr Minted patted Rex, their Afghan hound.

"Of course he's a dog!" said Mum.

Mr Minted smirked. "No ... this is a real dog," he boasted. "Look at its long, silken hair. Magnificent! Look at yours. Not a hair in sight. Ha ha!"

Mum glared at Mr Minted, and Sue and Gary patted Chip protectively.

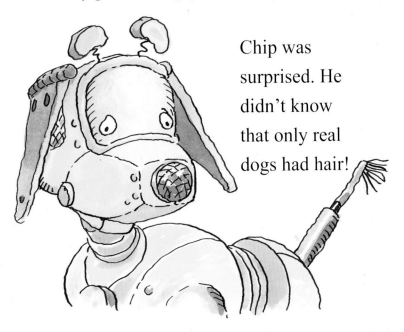

Chip was surprised. He didn't know that only real dogs had hair!

With his nose in the air, Rex came into the garden and walked regally towards them.

"A-a-a–" Dad began to sneeze. With a hankie to his nose he rushed into the house.

"Hello, boy," said Sue and Gary, patting the big dog.

"Aren't you lovely?"
murmured Sue.
"You've got a beautiful
coat."

Rex yawned.
He'd heard all
this before.

"Yes. What a dog!" said
Gary, stroking its back.

"What a dog!"
agreed Sue.

"Right you are,"
sneered Mr
Minted. "A real
dog. Not like that
thing of yours.
That's not a dog, that's a tin can on legs!"

He and his wife snorted with laughter.
"Come on, Rex," Mrs Minted called.
"It's time for your
appointment at the
Pet's Beauty Parlour."

Mr and Mrs Minted left and Chip hung his head. He didn't like being called a tin can. He wanted to have hair and be called a real dog.

"The Minteds are always like that, Chip," said Sue as Mum went indoors, fuming. "Just ignore them."

"Come on, we'll go for a walk!"

But Chip stared at the ground.

"Maybe he'd like to play," said Gary and fetched his football.

But the robodog turned his head away. He didn't feel like walking or playing. He was wondering where he could get some hair.

If only he could get some hair then Gary and Sue would say, "What a dog!"

Sue tried again.

"Chip ... fetch!"
she cried and
threw a stick.

The robodog didn't move.
"What's wrong, Chip?" Sue asked. "Are
you OK?"

Gary frowned. "Maybe he doesn't know what to do ...

Like this, Chip," he said, and fetched the stick himself.

Still Chip didn't move.

"Let's take him indoors," said Sue. "Maybe he feels cold out here."

They went into the living room where
Dad was watching a detective film.

The robodog glanced at the screen and
his ears swung up.

A robber was waving a big stick around.
"Drop it! This is the police!" shouted
the detectives.

"Look, Chip likes TV!" said Gary, and
Sue smiled as she saw that the robodog
was watching the film.

"Drop it!" the detectives yelled again.
"This is the police!"

Gary and Sue sat down to watch the movie but Chip was now more interested in what he saw in the street.

Mr Minted was taking Rex to the Pets' Beauty Parlour.

Quietly Chip slipped out of the house
and followed Mr Minted and Rex.

He wanted to know
how Rex got his
lovely long hair.

Perhaps he
bought it at the
Beauty Parlour?

Pets' Beauty Parlour

½-price
nail-clipping.
A snip!

Hamsters
shampooed
while U wait

With your pet
had naturally
curly hair?
Give it a perm!

Chip watched as Mr Minted left Rex at
the Beauty Parlour.

He crept up to the
window, looked in
and stared in
amazement.

The people in the shop weren't giving
Rex more hair ... they were trimming
bits off the stuff he already had!

Chip was confused. What was going on?

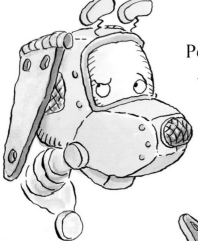

Perhaps some dogs with lots of hair gave some of it away to dogs who didn't have any.

Yes, that must be it!

Chip knew this was his chance. He
would go into the shop and get some
hair for himself. Then, when he was
hairy like Rex, Gary
and Sue would say,
"What a dog!"

He pushed open
the door and
went in.

An assistant was
standing with her
back to him.

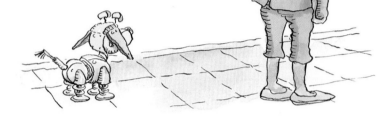

Chip stood up on his hind legs.

"Hello,"
he said in his
crackly voice.

The assistant
whirled round and
gasped.

"Aaah!" she cried.
"It's an alien!"

She sprayed the robodog with her can of
hairspray.

"Go away
horrible
spacethingy!"
she yelped.

"Get back to your own planet!"

The other assistant pointed her hairdrier
at the robodog and switched it on.

"You can't make me go on your flying
saucer!" she yelled.

The whoosh of air from the hairdrier blew a big cloud of Rex's hair over Chip.

The hairspray made it stick and suddenly ...

... the robodog
was hairy!

Rex blinked in
surprise. Where
had the strange-
looking dog come
from?

Chip saw himself in the mirror and
grinned in delight.
Now he was sure that Gary and Sue
would say,
"What a dog!"

He left the Beauty Parlour and trotted off down the street.

At the corner he stopped, looked around and sniffed the air. He had detected a familiar scent. It was the one that belonged to Gary's and Sue's dad ...

but he wasn't anywhere to be seen.

Then Chip saw where the scent was
coming from.

Lying on the
pavement not far
off was a wallet,
and the robodog
knew at once that it
must belong to
Sue's and
Gary's dad.

He was just about to fetch it when two
boys appeared.

One of them
picked up the wallet
and opened it.

"Look!" he
crowed. "Money!"
"Finders keepers!"
cried the other.

"You're right," said the first and they
began to walk away.

Suddenly a deep voice boomed out.
"Drop it! This is the police!"

The boys stopped
in their tracks and
looked around
wildly.

All they could see was a funny little
hairy dog.
Suddenly the hairy little dog opened its
mouth.

"Drop it!" it said again. "This is the police!"

"Help!" yelped the boy with the wallet. "It's a talking police dog! Run for it!"

He dropped the wallet and the two boys took to their heels and fled.

Chip trotted over
to the walllet,
picked it up and
set off for home.

Meanwhile, Sue and Gary were
searching for him.

"Why do you think Chip ran away?"
said Gary as they hurried along.

"I don't know," Sue
replied. "I just hope
we find him."

Chip saw them coming
and stopped.
He was sure Gary and
Sue would like him
much better now that
he looked like Rex.

But Gary and Sue ran right on by.

"What a funny-
looking dog," said
Gary as they
passed.
"Very hairy," said
Sue.

Chip's head drooped.

Now he was sure
that Sue and Gary
didn't love him.

He trudged back to the house and went
into the living room.

Dad was still
watching TV.

Chip looked up at him.

Dad looked down
at Chip and gasped
in surprise.

"Whose dog are you?" he asked.

"Wha-wha-wha-
whaCHOOO!"
he sneezed and
blew the hairs off
the robodog's face.

Dad blinked. "It's Chip!" he cried as Mum came in.

"You're back!" she said in delight. "Wonderful!"

Dad looked at the hairs all over Chip's body.

"But why is he so hai-hai-hai-

haaaACHOO!

he sneezed again and blew off the rest
of the hairs.

Just then Sue and Gary
came running in.

"Oh, Chip, where have you been?" cried
Sue, giving him a big hug.
"And why did you run away?" asked
Gary, stroking him.

Mum smiled and picked up some of the
hair from the carpet.

"This is Rex's, if I'm not mistaken," she said. "It looks like Chip has been to the Beauty  Parlour too. My guess is he wanted to be like Rex and look like a real dog."

Sue gave Chip another hug.

"You don't have to be like Rex," she said. "You're just perfect as you are!"

"You're brilliant," said Gary. "And you're ours!"

"You don't have to be hairy to be a real dog, you know," said Dad.

"Personally, I'm delighted that you have no hair!"

Chip was overjoyed.
He liked being this
family's dog.

It was then that Gary noticed Chip was
holding something in his mouth.

"What have you
got there, Chip?"
he asked.

"Woof!" barked Chip and the wallet dropped from his mouth.

"Look at this!" exclaimed Dad, picking it up. "Chip found my wallet!"

He patted the robodog and grinned from ear to ear. "What a dog!" he said.

"What a dog! Wait till I tell the Minteds how clever he is."

Mum, Gary and Sue laughed and patted
Chip too.
"What a dog!" they all cried.

The robodog grinned in delight and
stood up on his hind legs.
"Hello," he said.